For Maya, who gave me my voice.

I, the Rock, I the River, I the Tree
I am yours—your Passages have been paid.

Lift up your faces, you have a piercing need
For this bright morning dawning for you.

-Maya Angelou

Table of Contents

The Rock (The Territory of Being Black)

The Tree: Courage

The River: MOMENTS.

The Spirit: Poetry for the Soul

Forward

Dear Reader,

My creative journey with Lester began back in 2017 when he submitted one of his works to a Black History Month zine anthology I had been compiling at the Sojourner Truth Library in New Paltz, NY. The poem he submitted, "This How I Talk," is about the stigma many poets face when they have unique, often ethnic voices. By the end of the experience editing Lester's poem, it became clear that the interaction itself was a manifestation of the poem's underlying message: Poetry—all writing—has the power to transcend systematic constraints (including "proper" English grammar). The process of helping Lester to hone his unique voice and strategically edit his poetry was equally as fulfilling for me as it had been for him. When he asked me to mentor him as he worked on his project for the Sillins Scholarship, it was not a difficult decision to accept his request.

Throughout this experience, we delicately navigated the editing process together in order to truly honor Lester's voice while effectively communicating his messages to readers in a way that reflects his performance poetry style. In my office, Lester performed his poems for me tirelessly as I matched the words on his pages to the words he spoke. Lester's poetry has a rhythm synonymous with his heartbeat, with his breath. His messages are raw. They are honest. When you read them, you will feel them in your bones. Lester not only created a 100-poem manuscript, but he is in the process of creating a collaborative accompanying album – His work is multifaceted and dynamic. I highly recommend catching the live show on May 10, 2019 at the Denizen Theatre.

I feel privileged to have had the opportunity to mentor Lester throughout the production of *100 Poems for 100 Voices,* and I look forward to seeing what other world contributions are in his future. Thank you, Lester, for teaching me just as much as I have taught you. May our creative journey never end.

Sincerely,
Charlene V. Martoni-McElrath

Preface

The language that made me a poet derived from shit like this—

Black Mama's No-nonsense Social Doctrine, Verse 3:19
"How many times I gotta tell yo' ass to get up and do these dishes?"
"'Tired,' my ass. If you don't get yo' black ass up…"

It came from Saturday mornings
Pots banging along to the wake-up sound of Frankie Beverly's "Before I Let Go."

It came from the third amendment
"I'm not one of ya little friends," written in the
Don't Try Me Or You'll Get Yo' Ass Whooped Bill of Rights Edition

It came from
"Stay outta grown folks' business and stay in a child's place."
(The Warning)

It came from
"I don't want ACS knocking on my door. Have yo' ass in this house before that clock hit 6." Translation: *I don't want anything to happen to you, baby.*

It came from the steps of Brooklyn
Kids playing in the rain and sunshine
While ice cream trucks sang nursery rhymes…
"Ashes, ashes, we all fall down."

It came from
"What happens in this house stays in this house.
So what Uncle Ronny did to you
Ain't that big of an issue."

This is the language that made me a poet.

—Lester

Acknowledgments

This offering of poetry, the varying untold stories with the common thread of humanity would not be possible without my Love Village, all of whom have raised, taught, encourage, believed and have loved me when I needed to be loved. This is the only way I could ever say "thank you." This is the only way I could truly say "I love you, too."

You see, at first when I began this journey I did not feel worthy of it; I felt that there was no way this could be done by me, and done right. But then, I thought about all of you and realized that all of our stories deserve to be told, and the universe deserves to acknowledge our existence. Then, I realized that it no longer was about it being done *right*, but about it being *truthful*.

All of the advice, tears, laughter, gathering together at dinner tables, dancing 'till four a.m. on the streets in Mississippi, marching in Manhattan, *loving* in Brooklyn, exploring in Ireland, being loved by many as a brother, son, uncle, nephew and even sister, aunt and muva has come full-circle — in this book, between every line and every punctuation.

Thank you to all the individuals from Public School 5, Urban Assembly Academy for Business and Community Development, Urban Assembly School for the Performing Arts and West Side High for always being a vessel of encouragement and the foundation of my creativity.

To my professors, counselors, and staff at Finger Lakes Community College and SUNY New Paltz, thank you for helping me open doors beyond my imagination.

To all my Villagers that stay up late on the phone with a smile while lending me their ears and talking me through the hardships and loving me back to myself, I love you, thank you.

Thank you to the Sillins Scholarship for funding all of my research and believing in my poetry.

Thank you to Nicholas Aiezza for encouraging me to pick up the pen when I thought I was the weakest writer in this world. Thank you for changing my perception on writing, and thank you for introducing me to the sounds of Nina Simone.

To my sister-friend, editor and mentor Charlene, thank you for hearing my voice and for honoring it as an editor and a lover of poetry. Thank you for teaching me what I needed to know.

To Liz and Bradley thank you for wrapping me in your arms and showing me many ways to achieve and encouraging me.

To my sisters, friends, cousins, we are conquering this world together and it is up to us to change it and make space where they said "there's no room." I love you all so much. I could not have done it without you, and this book is not only for you, but your children and their children.

To Bonnie, Chris, Mike and Lynnda, thank you for loving and supporting me. Thanks for being family.

Thank you to my family.

"It is so important that all artists remain obedient to their craft and surrender to it whenever it calls. Because, one day, someone somewhere will need that message to hang onto — or the artist themselves might need it when they no longer believe in art.

Stop waiting, and create.

Trust the truth."

-Lester

1

The Rock:

(The Territory of Being Black)

Pathology

In Africa, during the commencement of the slave trade,
A STRONG, BRILLIANT, BLACK MAN
Known 'round the village as someone's:
Father, brother, uncle, cousin, and husband
Chained, locked and bound people of his reflection, handing them off to invaders
In exchange for currency with Hopes of dodging slavery
When in reality
He traded in his history.

On the corners of the NYC drugs infestation,
A STRONG, BRILLIANT, BLACK MAN
Known 'round the hood as somebody's:
Father, brother, uncle, cousin, and husband
Advertised, enabled and traded off dope to people of his reflection
In exchange for currency in Fear of becoming a druggie
When in reality
He, too, traded in his history.

Turkey Sandwich

The word
"Picnic"
Often accompanies the early 1900 phrase
"Pick a nigger"

Like little Amy saying

"Billy, let's go watch that nigger boy get hanged—
But don't forget the blanket and Turkey sandwich
Because without it
It wouldn't be the same."

Sweet Meat

During slave times
White masters
Poured sugar
Into the open wounds of gay slaves

Birthing the phrase
"Sugar in his tank."

Where the Black Boy Lies

A white woman
Tall as the morning sun
With no license to disobey the laws of tomorrow
Is awoken at 4:30am by the sheriff of
Birmingham Alabama.

He says to her:

"Now, Miss Ida, I don't want no trouble,
But folks down yonder told me they saw a young
Negro boy running through here.
Now,
They say he winked and touched the hand of the Congressman's wife
And we've been tryin' to locate and talk to him since last night.
Have you seen him, ma'am?"

She clears her throat
Pushes up her privileged voice
Pulls back her shoulders, lengthens her neck, grips the door knob

And says:

"One day I will die,
But until that day comes
That is all that I will do for death.
You see, I'll die long before I tell anybody
Where the black boy lies."

Enough

It wasn't until they were dragged across water wetter than tears
Stood on auction blocks wedded with African biddings that

Harriet pulled the rifle up off her back
Rosa refused and sat
Maya wrote
Maxine spoke
Eric choked

That they realized
Peace in America could never be still
And America will never be still in peace

Talk About It!

In the beginning was the word
And the word was "faggot"
And the word was "hell"
And the word was "all faggots go to hell"
And the word was "all hell here come these faggots"

Didn't they know better?
Didn't they have no shame?
Don't they?

In the beginning was the word
And the word was "nigger"
And Nigger became "Nigga"
And the final words was "matter."

And the word was "all niggas matter except those faggots"

Is they serious?

If

If Sandra made it home safe
She would've gone to her new job and faced: sexism and racism head on in the work place

If Sandra made it home safe
She would've found a baby that needed love and taught them it had been inside them all along

If Sandra made it home safe
She would've blogged about the girls in Chicago who got shot by the cops and ignored by the block

If Sandra made it home safe
She would've written how Rosa feet were not tired, but Rosa was simply a Black woman who made the choice to stand out by sitting down

If Sandra made it home safe
She would've figured out that nobody was listening
That everyone was scared

If Sandra made it home safe she wouldn't have known how much she was loved.
Because
Nobody
Told her.

If Sandra made it home safe…

She shoulda
She coulda
She woulda

She
    Shoulda
        Coulda
            Woulda

Charlottesville, VA

He stands there

Crying on the inside!
Eyes puffy behind glasses
Clinched jaw as he hears the swirling ribbons
Of history:

      "You people"

"Boy"

          "Nigga"

              "Property"

      "Thugs"

HE
IGNORES
THEM

Holding onto a gospel song passed down from his grandmother,
In his heart and head he sings,

      "I
Shall
        Not
           Be
     Moved."

If God Ever Listened

"If God ever listened to poor colored women the world
would be a different place."
— Alice Walker's the Color Purple.

The heavy steps of a 6' 2" dark skinned black woman weighing in at 210 pounds
Rushed to the door and shouted
"Alice, make sure you come straight in after choir! Don't make me come down there!"

Quickly consumed by the heat that baked her skin by the minute,
Alice faintly turned to her and said, "Okay Mama, I ain't fixin to go nowhere else."

She took a deep breath
Daring down the dusty-dry roads of Money, Mississippi
The large amounts of sweat shampooed her hot-combed hair into an afro
Her crusty lips, which were moisturized with Crisco oil moments before leaving the house,
Now cried out for a glass of ice water.

Dazed out, leaning deeply into each side as she walked
No life appeared to be in her young-beautiful-big-brown-body.

Half-way through her journey
A red pickup truck swinging a confederate flag proudly like Yankees on the 4th of July
Slowed down and began driving alongside of her
 A voice rich with ignorance called out from the driver seat:
 "Look fellas, we done found ourselves a monkey in the heat."
One of the men on the passenger side laughed in discomfort
As the man in the back began making monkey noises.

She was horrified
She didn't look at them
She didn't scream
She didn't say "stop"
She couldn't.

She greedily clutched the hem of her dress and continued walking at normal pace.

Moments later the two men in front joined in
Making monkey sounds
And beating their chests.
The tires sped up, blowing dirt back on her as they flew down the road

Yelling "Monkey," "Nigger…"
Still, she continued walking at normal pace.

Thoughts of suicide dragged across her eyes,
Confusion from the heat tripped her voice and she shakily began singing at snail pace
Attuned to the southern heat:
"Oh Lord, I want two wings to veil my face. Oh Lord I want two wings to fly away. Oh Lord…"

The familiar early childhood invocations of "never good enough"
Interrupted her singing
Her eyes dropped to the ground
Still, she continued walking at normal pace.

Alice arrived at God's house where prayers pronounced her existence as worthy.
The excitement to sing for God, mixed with the relief of arriving safely,
Brought life back into her and carried her through the big wooden doors
Directing her footsteps towards the basement.

She began to prepare for youth choir rehearsal.
As always, she was the first one there
And took to the water fountain to cool her body.
With each sip she exhaled prayers asking God for forgiveness for those men.
She went into the bathroom and tried to position her hair in the fashions of Coretta Scott King. Staring in the
mirror, dusting off her freshly pressed dress, she heard three familiar voices…

Voices that were similar to hers:
Young, innocent, godly, curious, enduring the daily threats of their existence.
She heard the voices heading towards her and excitedly exited the bathroom to greet them,
"Sharon, Robyn, Cece! Oh my God, you won't believe what happen to me!"
And as the four girls leaned in for a group hug,
Pressing hearts together and kisses upon foreheads…

Time stopped.

Four black souls that had been paid for by their ancestors had been stolen.
 Hope for the future had been robbed:
The slick-talking poet full of potential
The mathematician to send a white man to the moon
The civil rights activist who would birth a bloodline of take-no-shit-negro's
And the voice that would sit between Billie Holiday, Ella Fitzgerald, and Sara Vaughn
Now laid voiceless and back-to-belly under wood
Just like their great, great grandparents who arrived on ships of darkness searching for light
A century earlier.

Outside of the four walls of the church... racism had won.

Every molecule of the bodies had exploded into pieces
Their skin burned into coal
And with a blink of an eye
With the quickness of a prayer
Everything those four girls could've—would've—become
Was completely erased
By the powerful
Ignorant
Hands of racism...

"Oh, Lord, I want two wings to veil my face.
Oh, Lord, I want two wings to fly away.
Oh, Lord, I want two wings to veil my face.
So, the devil won't do me no harm."

A Poem for Every Gay. Black. Feminine. Male.

Here's **our** story…

On Nov. 2nd,
14-year-old Giovanni Melton was killed by his father
Because he was acting "feminine."
When Giovanni's father asked him if he was gay,
He replied "yes."
His father replied by beating him
And shooting him in the chest.

I fear
That gay black feminine men
Will all die alone
That no time will come where someone will love us.

Instead,
They will run us down!
Beat us with bats!
They will set us on fire
Call us faggots in every language
In every tongue, from every religion.

Black Mothers will try to hide us while Black men cheer
Poets will use our experience to win trophies
Fire fighters will spray their water hoses on those that are Sweaty from playin' "faggot hunt."

Police officers will not come
Law makers will not come
Every traffic light will beam red
Every 'actorvist' will play dead

I fear
That Gay Black feminine men
Will all die alone
And

It won't be remembered like the Holocaust
Hell, it won't be touched upon like slavery
Children will not know of our existence
But will sing a nursery rhyme on our tomb-less grave
In exchange for good behavior.
There will be no obituaries,

No candles or flowers on the hour of our anniversary.

Mercilessly,
They will praise the days of Black gays
No longer existing—
A completed genocide mission.

I heard
Last week in Vegas a "father" beat his Gay Black son
Until he couldn't breathe
Beat until he could see
Beat until blood splattered between teeth

Heard, originally, he wanted to hang his ass
Yo' mother fuckers is triflin'
Heard, "He'd been plottin' on his demise since he came to the barbecue with a purse on"

Said he "waited for him at home all day"
Waited for him to look the wrong way
Waited for the reason to say
"He made me feel uncomfortable."

His father comfortably
Shot him dead in the chest.
He said
he'd "rather have him dead than gay."

I heard,
"I would've did the same shit."

Shit,
I guess Black lives only matter to straight Black folks—
Folks who don't believe in the Gay Black Existence
But will turn to us for our fashion opinion
Turn to us to babysit their children
Turn to us to decorate they' house they just bought down South.

I heard during the Civil Rights Movement there was
No room for homo behavior
I heard the oppressed Black folks
Kept those like *Bayard Rustin* out of history books
But behind pulpits advising *Dr. Martin Luther King*

Heard they was

Fine with him putting his life on the line
As long as that line lead straight to a closet
Straight into a grave without receiving any due.
I heard under the covers of night, in the trunk of a car,
He was evacuated from Montgomery
Because Black men where on a hunt for him
Because Black men wanted to hang him for being gay in that skin…

I know that till this day
Straight Black men will never come against a white gay man.
And will never-ever protect or celebrate Black Gay men
But will release their frustrations out on us then
Look for us to hold shit down
When the system has they're ass on lock down
So,

Instead of allowing history to repeat itself
Instead
Of waiting for that time to come

Instead
Of hoping that our bodies will no longer be
Stuffed in the trunks of cars

Use this time to take cover…
Get some practice
Find some space that's safe
So you won't be beat, raped, and left to rot for days
Barricade your doors...
Throw the blood of Leviticus on yo' windows
Scribble in script: "fuck you"
Delete every media that socially tracks you
Turn off yo' phones
Hold yo' guard!
Never sound the alarm...

Because they listenin'
They watchin'
They waitin'

I'm tellin you! It won't be safe for black femininity to exist
In any space in this lonely cold fucked up world come the day

When

28

We,
Prove
That Black Femininity, undeniably, is the strongest energy

In

The

World.

"Because rape on the body of a young person,
More often than not, introduces cynicism;
And there is nothing quite so tragic as a young cynic— Because it
means the person has gone
From knowing nothing to believing nothing."

-MAYA ANGELOU

Cynicism

Image by: Patrick Stelien

The rescue of the morning sun gazed upon his bruised,
Bloody black body kicking awake his reality.
Sounds of the semi-busy Brooklyn street tore through
The 2014 Aeropostale hoodie that covered his ears.

Buses screeching like screams of terror at midnight stopped to deliver
Plum, yellow, honey human beings whose voices mixed perfectly
With beeping horns and cultural madness.

Children's morning grunts and elders' morning prayers
Were thrusted upon passing strangers.
It was another day for him:
Another survived attack of selling his body to dick-gone-wrong.
Just hours earlier he trolled the back ends of Harlem looking for a John

Who choked and punched him dead in the eye after he requested his pay from a job well done.
After the brutal attack at the hands of a 'married straight man'
He hopped on the downtown C train on 116th Street leaking blood at 2:30 in the morning.

The hunger pains in his stomach and the fearful tremor that controlled his breath
Began to dissipate as he made his way towards Brooklyn,
A place where he knew no one would inquire about his face, well-being, and plights.
He would be invisible.
To him, invisibility meant safety.

Yawning and stretching through last night's disappointments
And confusion, he found the street-strength to grab his backpack from between his legs
And rush to the nearest Clean Rite Laundromat.

When he arrived, the owners were in back cleaning out dryers
And wiping down washing machines from the night before.
He snuck into the restroom and began his morning ablutions, reaching
Into his backpack and pulling out a thrice-stained, browned towel.

He rubbed the hard-dried blood off his face like winter snot on a 2-year-old child
And pulled out a wrinkled pair of brown pants
And a purple collared school shirt to costume his ashy body.
He sneakily exited the laundromat and treaded towards school
To make it in time for breakfast.

"Good morning, Ms. Johnson."
Ms. Johnson grunted at him, hinting at the usual disappointment
Of his wrinkled uniform and disheveled, untended-to skin and hair.
"Good morning Ujasiri, tuck in that shirt and put some lotion on."
Ujasiri laughed to himself.

Ms. Johnson was the closest thing to a mother he had.
She was a blunt, lightly toasted, buttered Black woman with short hair and glasses.
She could hear a fly landing against a wall in a room full of teenagers.

She spoke with the diction of God and had the arms of a noble Black woman who could
"Throw zown in the kitchen".

Students hated her ass; she was the law:
She treated everyone with the same respect and held them to the same standards
No matter how they presented themselves.
She was the Dean of Students, but in true Black Woman Fashion, she quadrupled as a:

Cook, therapist, pastor, and sometimes, doctor.
When she called home, parents knew she meant business.

The clock flew like tears on the face of a motherless child
That just received news of their morning turned mourning.
School was out, and now the biggest task was to stay low-key.
Afternoon warmth settled on the concrete, creating a fragrance of first-spring,

Children ran home or to after-school programs,

While Ujasiri headed to the library where he routinely did his homework
And read up on the greatest minds of literature, like:

Maya Angelou,

James Baldwin,

E Lynn Harris,

Edna St. Vincent Millay, and

Tennessee Williams.

He always had hope that he would be as great as them.
Inspiration ran through his mind,
Spinned down his finger tips, and dripped out his pen.

With unmitigated gall
He wrote:

"THE GRACE OF MORNING ALIGNED HIS FACE
EVENING FORMED HIS SMILES
MIDNIGHT COLORED HIS EYES
SURVIVAL SCRAPED HIS KNEES
THE PAINS OF LIFE SCARRED HIS WRIST
DEATH INTRUDED HIS MIND
FEAR OF LOVE STRUCTURED HIS SPINE
THE RESCUE OF THE MORNING SUN GAZED UPON HIS

BRUISED, BLOODY, BLACK SKIN

KICKING AWAKE HIS COURAGE TO BREATHE AGAIN."

"Was it necessary to shoot him?"

Mammie Till stood before the decomposing body
Her nostrils inflamed by the ordained smell of racism
His body had been chopped up by the grinding blades of ignorance.

Mammie Till said to the folks that came to comfort her
With the sweet potency of her slave history,
"Turn me a-loose, I don't have time to faint now,
I have a job to do."

No minister
No mother of the church
No scripture from the bible or lyrics from the Negro spirituals
Could prepare her eyes for what she was about to see.
"My lawd, my lawd, my lawd…"
Slowly as the coroner began to pull back the sheet
Mammie saw that his right eye was now laying on his cheek
His tongue had been choked out his throat
His teeth, left eye, and ears were gone.

Mammie realized he'd been split in the head to the bone
And like a window on her darkest day
Sun reign straight through the two bullet holes
That resided on what was once his temple

And the only thing she could think was:
"Was it necessary to shoot him?"

Mammie agreed to have an open casket
With the body untouched
The regurgitation of racism spit directly on America's dinner table
For all to turn away from.
`
Mammie was bodacious enough to send a message that not 100 speeches can send
That not 100 preachers can preach
That not 100 singers can sing
That not 100 sermons can hold—
Her baby was gone at 14 years old.

Black Cherries

Black bodies have polluted: oceans, rivers, and sewers—from slave times, 'till current times
Black bodies lie underneath brick high rise buildings in East Harlem
They make up the foundation of condominiums in Detroit
And are embedded in the redlining of the walls in the Mississippi court houses.

Back in the 1800s 'till now
200-pound Black men were hanged on trees
'Till their bodies rotted
'Till their weight couldn't wait for them to be cut down
'Till the lynch ropes snapped their necks, decapitating the tree.

It was said:
That the nigger body's sole purpose was for the fertilization of the Earth
That a nigger soul was only meant to live in soil
That Black bodies went from swinging on trees to birthing them.

Black bodies that have been fermented in the soil
Now grow:
Plumbs, melon, apples, and black cherries
For white women to pick, clean, chop up, bake, and consume
Then shit out.

The names of the Black souls that soil the **Strange** but familiar bruised **Fruit**
Will never be listed in the ingredients but,
They will warn you that throwing a banana peel in the recycling bin is not good for the planet.

Dammit I wonder
If they could taste the blood that pours through the pores of a lemon.
I wonder
If when they squeezed the lemon over their freshly fileted salmon if they understand
That history is repeating itself.

And I often think about
When Black people gather together to cook and celebrate under God's superstition
If they have any clue that the act of cannibalism lies
In every holy scoop of their banana pudding or is ordained in every bite of their candied yams
And every slice of their freshly picked sweet potato pie.

I wonder
If every time I walk passed a berry tree
Blowing in the winds
If my ancestors are trying to encourage me.

Home

She sent her baby down to the Delta,
Money Mississippi

The same way the Jews send their babies to
Jerusalem

The same way the Dominicans send their babies to the republic

The same ways the Ethiopians sends their babies to Ethiopia

The exact same way the Italians sends their babies to Italy

She sent her baby down to the Delta,
Money Mississippi

And unlike the Jew, the Dominican, the Ethiopian and The Italian
Her baby never returned home.

THE DOLL TEST:

It was painful to realize that I would never wake up from my dark, ugly nightmare.

That I would never see the new dawn break into a lighter me.

A lighter me with bluer eyes and blonder hair.

It's painfully true that I am stuck: black and ugly as ever.

Just like you.

911

"Just run,
Because if you don't.
You know how this ends up."

BlaQ

When a black boy enters a store
He must keep his hands in his pocket
He must stand at least 4 steps away from any merchandise
He must shop from a distance

He must smile while keeping his arms to his side
When he is asked "Do you need help?" for the 100th time
He must smile when he replies "No thank you"
He mustn't stay in the dressing room for too long
He must buy at least 75 percent of what he tries on
Too prove to the wrong
That he can rightfully afford it.

When a black boy shops he will be followed
He will be reminded of his displacement
When a black boy shops
He will buy
He will be sold
He will be freed
He will buy
And he will be sold again

A Poem for Sylvester James Jr

Nobody knows
Cause didn't nobody ask
Nobody dealt or wanted to be bothered with
Sylvester

A gay man whose pain ran longer and slower than the 6 train

Mother gone
Farther gone away
Always seeming to have to pay
A high price for love with receipts of loneliness

Nobody ever asked what it was like
Taking stages and bringing joy to the world
Beaming with tears when folks stand out of their comfort zones

The great feelings it brings
The intoxication you feel
When knowing keeping it real
Made them heal

"You're golden Sylvester"
"You're Beautiful"
"We love you"

He, not having like for himself, let alone love to give back

Went home, alone
To a dried-up toothbrush
A cold thick jar of Vaseline
A Stiff dry towel
And a bed that ain't been visited for seven months

A sparkly dark community birth him
But he stole away to shine mightier
Than he was allowed to

He walked high
He had so much to give

And once found someone to give it to
But AIDS came and stole him away

Iatrophobia

Iatrophobia which means fear of the healer. It derives from the Greek word "iatric,"
Meaning or relating to a specified kind of medical practice.

"Iatric." Like "Psychiatric."
Like Black mother saying,
"Something's wrong, child, but don't worry about the rape you endured
Just put on that Kirk Franklin song and pray along."

Like "Pediatric."
Like Black mothers dying
From giving birth in the hospitals at 11.5 percent higher rate than any other race.

Like "Iatraliptic."
Like, "Don't need no medicine
Ain't about to pay for something that Advil can do,"
Even though it might leave you with damage tissue.

Iatrophobia.

Delta

Take me to the water
Where the tears haven't dried up
Where the snots and sweat of confusion are buried beneath the sea
Where the rivers have pretty names like: Sunflower and Sawn
And hold tales like the Tallahatchie
Take me to the water because

I'm here

Here in Mississippi and
My heart, is heavy
My throat, filled with apology
My eyes crusted with sympathy
And all I could think about is water.
Bodies of
Water.

Drown me.

Black ain't just one thang.

It don't always show up
With an afro and a fist
It don't always play hip hop,
Blues, Jazz, and R&B
It's all of that and then some

You wouldn't even believe it:
It' aint always straight
It's also bisexual and gay
And then some

It's not just a man/woman,
cis or trans—it's neither.
It just is!
Just is.

Black wakes up and goes to sleep
It speaks French, Spanish, Japanese, and Swahili

Black eats fried chicken, watermelon, salad, and beats.

Black fights for the right of every working person.

Black is called: Egypt, Florence, China, and Queen

Black is all of this,
But according to them
It's supposed to be divided upon skin tone,
Sexuality, and language
Limited upon limits…
Isn't it?

An Ode to the Sounds of Blackness

When Ray Charles asked, "Come live with me and won't you be my love?"
Gladys said she's leaving to be with him
On a midnight train to Georgia
Aretha politely demanded, "Will you call me the moment you get there?"
And Toni Braxton responded with, "Maybe…"
John Legend said he'll think about it
And Aretha circled back around with "You better think."

The black sound started a war between the East and West
While leading thousands from the South to freedom.
The black sound is the culture/the revolution/the solution, and the bigotry.
If we say "No more," the soul of America will cease to exist.

The Negro spirituals didn't stop with the blues, and the blues didn't stop with Hip Hop.
Only those in touch will recognize the pattern…
The same cry, the same wants, the same needs,
Just written-spelled-out-and-delivered differently.

Biggie said, "It was all a dream"
And Meek added a "nightmare," too.
After Teddy said it was time to wake up
Soul II Soul regulated us
Back To Life Back To Reality.

The Black Sound is a parody of our prefect destiny.
That's why everyone was so confused when
When Mary sanged she was going down
And Erykah gave her "three dollars and six dimes…"

It was such a contradiction when
One black woman said, "I can't stand the rain"
And another sanged, "Go on and let the rain pour"
But
LaShun Pace cried, "There's a leak in this old building and my soul has got to move"
Luther Vandross giggled with, "Good, 'cause a house is not a home"

Everyone, still confused, turned to
The Education and The Miss replied
"Lauryn is only human"
So they turned to Nas, and he offered One Love
Enticing CeeLo to holler, "Fuck you."

When Marvin asked, "What's going on?"
Alicia had to tell the truth with Karma

In the name of the Black Sound
Miley Cyrus *twerks*
Justin Timberlake *rifts*
And Christina Aguilera holds all her *syllables*.

While Beyoncé rings The Alarm of Formation, Sam Cooke
Suggests, it seems like A Change Is Gonna Come and Sweet Etta James, relieved, exhales
With, "At Last…"
The black sound is the only sound that will save America
Shhh…
Listen closely.

2

The Tree:
Courage

From the Bottom of Freedom

"Yesssss, Bitch!"
Voguing to the underground beats
Barbequing steak and beef
Drinking Amaretto Sour
Nodding along to masculine power:

I slide off my du-rag
Fasten up my wig
Waiting for the next phobic man to tell me
All about his

Truths about God…Lies about hell
I'll laugh and swear I might end up in jail
If he don't carry that bullshit
Down to that bar where
Drag Queens ain't allowed to shine
Or purge like a star

On this block and in this house
There's enough room for All Queens

To show up and show out and glitter
Just like Queen B.
So, carry on Miss RIRI

I see you, Queen Jante
Talk that shit, Maxine Waters
I'm Living! Janelle Monae!

All Queens, each induvial,
Sharing one thing deep in their tissue:

Havin' clawed our way to freedom, gotten knocked back down and beaten.
Still, from the bottom of freedom with glitter and sass! And a bare-naked ass
We gladly ask:

Aint we fab?
And
Aint we fine?

Aint we fine?
And
Aint we fab?

Yes Gawd, Bitch!
And if they ain't
Shiit, I know I am!

Yes, I switch when I walk
I unconsciously sing when I talk
I can walk down the street minding my own business
And hear someone, somebody saying some fucked up shit to me
I can just take it as an insult, but if I say anything to someone
About something I'm feeling
It could be the end
Of my life.

I can walk away from ignorance and still be human
But they cannot
Without losing dignity, which is aesthetically acceptable.
The dependency of my staying alive
Relies heavily on my acts
But, yes, sometimes gays are extra
For a lot of reasons.

Aint we fab?
And
Aint we fine?

Aint we fine?
And
Aint we fab?

Mistaken Identity

Even when she was straight
And pretended to date
Men
She knew, something was missing

Even when he peed
He didn't approve of what was between his
Knees
He knew, something was missing

Something, they closed the gates of heaven for.

Choir

When a Trans woman is smacked across the face, she cries
When a young feminine boy is smacked on his scalp then told to "act right" he cries
When a baseball player dared to love exclusively and got his heart broken abruptly, he cries
When a grandmother must comfort her child that is burying their seed, she cries
When a parent is told, "you are not my real parent," they cry
When a drug addict gives over their kids in exchange for a hit they cry
When a child awakens in a warehouse longing for mommy and daddy's hand for warmth they cry
When a rich woman spits on her maid for being forgetful, she cries
When a niece sees her uncle, who raped her, and is forced to give him a hug,
She tucks her eyes and cries.

I wonder what it would sound like if we all listened and heard
Ourselves harmonizing on the same cry.

Slow Ride to The City

This poem is for the folks who believe sterling silver is the highest they can go
And that gold is only a fairytale told by the rich.

This poem is for them same folks who don't believe that love is any type of wealth
But understand that loneliness is the greatest payment of karma, at least that's what they believe.

This poem is for the artist who rides the A Train
Giving divine dance for three minutes and 22 seconds
Between 42nd and 125th street — A glorious show worth up to 150 dollars per person
But accepts pocket change, smiles, fist bumps and handshakes.

This poem is for black people that are only nice to white people.

This poem is for the once rape victim who is now the rapist.

This poem is for 10 years ago
10 months ago
10 days ago
10 hours ago
10 minutes ago
10 seconds ago

This poem is for everyone
For we are all killing ourselves
Trying to stay alive.

Innocence

Sometimes monsters are real.
Sometimes life changes you for the worse.

When life puts a straw up to its lips and blows out a rape,
It also blows out the promises the future once held—far out into the distance.

Sadly, for some folks, life blows out more traumas than one can handle.

Innocence can be lost/stolen even.
Innocence can be found...reimagined
Even.

Can it?

"Yes, for SOME people."

Hard Pill to Swallow

They say every five-to-seven years your taste buds change
They must
You see
At 7 years old
I began loving men that reminded me of the men that raped me.
At 14
I swirled into the down lowe world and began living for men that kept me private.
At 21
I measured myself growing in love with a man that respects and cherishes me.

So, I thought

Believe Me

If I could:
Unabandon you
Un-rape you
Un-neglect you
Un-birth you
Love you
I would.

Nite Time

Dat man momma bought home last week
Comes in and out my room every night
He says he's checking for monsters
He says he trynna make sure I'm all right
But his fingers wake me in places that don't feel nice
I don't say anything to mama
Cause she say I'm "always a problem"
And plus, mama saw him come in one night
And didn't stop him or put up a fight.

Journal Entry 6/22/18:

I've been more private
Protecting what's left of me

I've been softer with me
Slower with me

Taking daily inventory
Finding what needs to be found—and I've found

That I've learned not to make the:
Current job I'm working
School I'm attending
Lover I'm loving
Weight I'm carrying
Skin I reside in
Religion I abide in

All of me

But it's so hard to be
Because truthfully,
I refuse to be lonely.

But She Doesn't

She lost two of her babies in the 70's to crack
In the 80's her husband got stabbed in the chest and bled to death
In the 90's her only sister jumped off a building in the middle of the crowded city of Baltimore.
Today, like a washing machine carrying a load too big
She breaks down
Every morning she rises
She thinks about ending it.
But she doesn't.

What's the joke?

Sitting in class, feeling, unbearably embarrassed.
The joke of the room is written down in her stomach and it reads
"Young and pregnant."
Students laugh, teachers gasp
"shame on her"
"girl couldn't, wouldn't be me"
"Poor child, she use to be a smart girl"

Sitting in the doctor's office, laughing, hysterically.
The joke of the room is written down in her stomach and it reads
"Unfortunately, you will never be able to conceive."
People stare as she fills her belly with air
Trying to *feel* what it would feel like to be free.

Still, laughing hysterically.
Still, unbearably embarrassed.

For Mississippy

Nobody checks in anymore
On the kid living on the fifth floor

The one whose mamma works all day
And father limps with a cane for pay

Nobody makes sure the kid gets home safe
All they do is send him to the sto' for cigarettes
But never offers him the change

Nobody checks his report card
Or hang up his science awards
Nobody asks him to play ball

All he does is sit at home all day and wait for mamma to get in to ask about her day
"In a minute son"
As if he's complaining

Nobody sung happy birthday to him
Or brought him a plate for Thanksgiving or
Made him a scarf for Christmas and didn't bother to tell him when a New Year came in
And because he believed he was Nobody

It all made sense when somebody found him hanging
Everybody grieved and couldn't believe that nobody bothered to check in
On the boy living on the fifth floor
And damn it's too late
He don't need y'all no mo'

But do you remember the days when people would die
And sweet folks would send cake and pie
And lay hands on the afflicted soul to pray
For comfort under the hard times and grief that's on its way.

Now is not the time to Quit.

When it rains like a hurricane
When it snows like no tomorrow
When it's pitch dark in the park
When you hear mean screams
When innocence is reported missing
When
    you
       find
          out
            happiness
                    is
                     not
                        the final stage of life.
Is the divine time when an artist MUST go to work.

First Aid

I am not a quick scrape on the knee
I do not heal quickly
I scar easily
I am an open wound that must be sewn back together
(Old-fashioned way with thread and needle)
Then
Rubbed with ointment
Then bandaged
Then
After 12 hours you must remove my bandages and give me space to breath
For I am not
A quick scrape on the knee

Who?
My thighs are thunder
My ass skips like rock thrashing across a lake
My hips sway like highway sign in a strong breeze
My piss splash like champagne

I am God

My feet are hard like metal
My ankles roll like dice
My knees are strong and watered like melon
My chest bends at night

I am human

Work Ain't Honest But…

It seems like everything and everyone gets to voice their opinions about me, but me.

The clock tells me when I should move on and how quickly
The bed lets me know when to lay, how to lay, and if I can lay safe
The shadows in the hallway alert me when I must prop myself up
And surrender over to danger

Food, rent, liquor and weed makes sure
The breaking, the robbing and the abandoning of my broken hole
Is my only claim to survival

Not because I *cain't* do anything else.
Nah, because I *cain't* be anything else,

I'm an artist
But that don't pay the bills
And you better damn well better believe if I'm gonna work for a man
It's gonna be on my time, my dime, and creatively.
And I don't really care who don't like it.

My downstairs neighbor always gives me a skanky look when we greet in the lobby
She reminds me of my mother: old, bitter, and won't ever offer any help
Only judgment and disapproval

Well, that don't work for me so I smile at the cranky bitch and carry on about my day

Quiet as it kept,
I think about if that old lady and mama would meet.

They'd probably, foolishly disagree about
The sky being blue,
That chicken should never be fried with an egg
And that a new born babe should always be breast-fed

But I guarantee

The only thing they would agree on is
Me
Being a skank, slut, fag and everything else to be ashamed of
And I would agree

Yes,
Me
My opinion
I would

Because I'm painfully proud of me.

Waking Up is Painful

It's putting your alarm on,
Not hitting the snooze button when it rings,
Removing the cover to reveal the sun light,
Clenching to the front of the bed dreading the wooden floors,
Putting one foot down on the ground at a time,
Heading over to the sink to wash away your mask, brush your teeth, lotion your body,
Putting your pants on, finding a decent shirt, sliding on your socks, then your shoes,
Grabbing your coat, scarf, hat and gloves if need be,
Taking a deep breath, opening the door, *locking it behind you,*
Walking slowly
Or quickly
As you dare
To love yourself
To therapy.

3

The River:
MOMENTS.

Medicine

(For when you need it)

Have you ever gone into a kitchen to fix yo' self a cup of hot coffee,
And while sprinkling in some sugar
Tears poured into yo' glass instead of cream?

Sometimes my back hurts from standing
My knees hurt from bending
My ankles swell from walking
My jaw aches from clenching
But most times,
Usually,
Routinely,
At 9pm
My heart breaks from loneliness.

Life is never too rough,
Too hard, or impossible
It is only 'us' who believe we are unable to dare it
To live it
To find beauty in death of relationships
To have enough time to live
Enough courage to believe
Life is not that hard.

The easier things get easier
The harder things get harder.
Maybe it's not that difficult
Maybe you do know
Maybe it's time to trust yo-self.

Maybe.

And say out loud:
"I am not the Backbone.
I am the Body."

He's got the whole world in his hands
He's got the whole world in his hands
He's got the whole world in his hands
And he separates parents and children

Dear Child,

I see you won't smile unless I'm around.
If I could take you home with me

I would. I promise you.
It's going to get better.

I'm sorry

Going through some shit?

Mad at the world?

Guess What?

Can't Guess?
Here's a clue:
It's not only happening to you!

You will miss me most
When I only exist inside your heart
You will call me most
When you say a prayer
You will love me most
When you look at our pictures
And weep.

The word
"Society"
Is an excuse.

A divider.
A reason to *not* understand:
What, how and why you're able to sleep peacefully at night.

While children are bombed, forced on bloody knees in warehouses
Covered in nothing but pain and confusion.

To smile
Is to live
To live is to understand
Every single grownup was once a child
And every child will learn that children are not immune to terror.

Hurt Children
Grow up
Scared adults
Never forget

Cook your food
To nourish your body
Seduce yo' taste buds
Make love with water
Birth appreciation
And know it's not
A conspiracy to have clean air you don't see

Love
Is
Not
A
Gift
From
Your
'God'

But
The
Gift
Of
Love
Is
Your
God.

The seven-year-old stares at his reflection in a broken mirror and sees you.
Do you smile back?
Can you honestly say that he's not you?
He thinks you're him.
What do you do?
Turn your head quickly to see if he'll follow?
Touch the broken glass to see if his hands move?
Or stand, still hoping he'll blow away?
Answer me?!
I'm staring at **you**.

I wish humans can figure out a creative way to live in peace
To live amongst each other with no Tyranny
The same way squirrels, birds and bees live amongst trees in peace.

If we think cats are evil
And dogs are stupid

I wonder what they think about us.

No post from
Beyoncé
Rihanna
Nicki
Cardi
And other Queens to come
Can make you love yourself

Only:
Time
Honesty
And **necessary breakdowns**
Can do that.

We've seen proof of hope many times before
Each time we've leaned in to touch it
And we've fucked it up.
Every time.

Death is like a fierce wind blowing through a cracked window
At the most inopportune times in life
Knocking down a familiar book that sits upon a wooden brown shelf
Embroidered with ghostly dust
Revealing dreaded pages holding names of angels and devils
Long gone
Gone too soon and
Soon to be reborn

When you burry me, I will rise with you in the morning.
The dead belongs to us, too.

I tend to run when I'm scared
I run to new places
With new people
And feel safe.
Being safe
Scares me
So I run.

Whew,
My Feelings Are Sore.

A
New
Born
Baby
Does not have long to wait for death.

Especially when she's labored from the grave unannounced.

P.S.
How? does a child
Playing in the park
Just before dark
Equate
To the wrong place?

I'm tryna figure out in my mind
How? it could be the wrong time.

Allowing names of slave owners, violators,
And any other human being who couldn't use their constructions for good
To be glorified in institutions, in text books, social doctrines, and on buildings
Where "all are welcome"
Is dangerous.

It is the brick that holds the door open for unnecessary ignorance to seep through.

When one walks and slips on water or trips on uneven concrete
It is easy to suggest that the lesson to be learned is to stay aware of your surroundings:
Put on water boots when it rains
And take bigger steps when walking the streets.

But when a violation occurs on the body of innocence,
It is the truth of a straw weighing down because the camel forgot its strength,
The world spins off its axis because gravity gives up,

"The child gives, because the body can, and the mind of the violator cannot"
-Maya Angelou

4

The Spirit:
Poetry for the Soul

One At a Time they came in and took their turns on me. Separately, each induvial introduced a new proclivity. With every belt jingle and draws dropping I braced myself to never breathe again, and wished for the blessing of *death* in that moment. One at a time, they repeated with each stroke, "Yea, take it. Faggot ass, stop frontin' like you don' like that shit." Each insult was underscored with a giggle from the violators in line awaiting their turn.

All seven of them sweaty, with identical masks on, and different smells. Distinctively, (from what I could remember) number three smelt like a Macy's clothing store around the holidays and number five smelt like; old wood, mothballs, and old lady perfume, as if he had come straight from bible study.

I fell out into a blackness and empty thoughts invaded for a moment; I don't remember much or know where I went. Nor do I want to. But when I came to, I opened my eyes and my bottom and mouth was sore from the tearing and forcing. The seven men, now crowded around me as their shadows shone down on me, their moans increased, their breathing became heavier, their bodies dripped and each sweat drop fell faintly. The sounds of flesh being lathered with large amounts of Vaseline increased. The seven men took turns, circling around me like a moving conveyer belt, sprinkling their DNA on my body. It felt baptismal.

Each one of them shook their large penises dislodging any excess poison of pleasure. They got what they needed. I got what I deserved, I supposed. I found myself praying, thinking about friends and family, and wondered if anyone would come to save me? And if I told, would they ever believe me?

"Get up!" one of them said. Holding no other option, I stood and the quickly drying sperm began to slide down my eye brows, lips, chest and thighs. "You liked that?" I replied, "yes," I couldn't say no. If my tears and pleading them to "stop" didn't convey my experience, it was clear by the delivery of the question I had one answer, and one answer only. The guy behind me commanded, "Yo, hurry up and get dressed." I quickly reached for my pants now blinded by the sperm sitting heavy on my eye lids.

I was somewhere else in my mind and I didn't even notice blood sliding down my inner thighs. It wasn't until I slid my left leg in my black jeans that I noticed the "Waist 29" on the white tag had been blurred and dyed devil red. Each leg lift felt as if I had boulders for ankles. One at a time they said in many variations, "You bet not say nothing. I' know where you live, little nigga." I said nothing and swallowed the little bit of spit in my mouth, it slid down like rocks. "If you like it, we might be able to arrange something." I held on to every word they spoke, every whisper, every tone, I tattooed their voices, threats and pleasures into my brain. I'll never forget it.

I limped out of that house empty handed and empty minded. The sun had yet to rise up and I knew, if I walked fast enough, I could make it in time for breakfast. I treaded back to the group home. That was the last time I snuck out in the middle of the night. That was the last time I went somewhere with someone, I thought I could trust.

SORRY (For Fie, Shan and Fish)

Dear Sister

I apologize for looking you alive in your eyes
And not reminding you that I love you

Of all the things that make
My heart beat
My sleep peace
My joy peak

You, my sister, are the reason
I traveled across bloody rivers
Without the talent to swim
So I can make it to the end
And breathe in the joy
Levitate in my sleep
And feel the heartbeats life earned me.

Sister, I left you behind in fear I wouldn't make it
Sister, I left you behind with the mission to save you

But Sister, these next lines might be real hard

Real hard for you to understand:

"You did not need me to save you, Sister.
All you needed was your hand,
your eyes, your simile,
your anger, your energy,
The little you might fear,
The most you might gain—
'You,' alone. You."

So, I don't regret leaving you, sister

I only regret not saying "I love you."

For Maya and Momma.

Hey Dr. Angelou

I would imagine had my mother lived past three years after giving birth to me
Her songs would sound so godly. Just like you.
Her words would spray like perfume. Just like you.
Her cry would bring alive every child born still and gone. Just like you.
Her hands would throw down on any man like a heavy weight champ. Just like you.

I would imagine had she been here she would dare
To love a child that lives out loud and PROUD. Just like you.

Like you,
I know she's now wrapped up in the core of the earth
Still hurt at the way the world works.
I can hear y'all laughing together at our panics
Knowing it'll get better because the world has gone through worse.

I heard from a man who stands on corners
That he heard from the people who weep for hell
That chances are heaven is small.
So, I know when ya'll got there
They had to make a little extra room for you.

Momma, Maya
Oh god, I love you.

Somebody

Has anybody ever told you how much we need you
Has anybody ever suggested that when you wake up in the morning you must be delicate with yo' self
Has anybody ever cupped a prayer and poured it over your body for protection
Has anybody ever recorded your voice and played it back again and again and again in awe of your language
Has anybody ever told you that you are worth respect and great hospitality whether you are being served or are the server
Has anybody ever made you feel like a human being
Like you are somebody
Somebody worth living and loving and laughing and crying.

This poem has been brought to you by Somebody
Who struggles to love themselves daily but found enough courage to love you, too.

My Home in Georgia

One morning I will wake up in my big, beautiful, colorful home and head to my kitchen and prepare a soulful dinner: honey butter corn bread, southern macaroni and cheese, fried chicken, salmon croquettes, macaroni salad, potato salad, fresh garden salad, collard greens; and for dessert, two cheesecakes, one triple chocolate cake, and three sweet potato pies.

And the greatest minds of My Time:

Mariel
Mo
Cat
Imani
Maayan
Samantha
Gerlando

You

Will ring my bell, come inside, sip sangria and sit at my table, say grace for the world, and enjoy.

We might write truths and tell lies
Or we might roll up, chill, and breathe easy.
Make history

We might figure out some shit:
An end racism
A cure
Love

We might.

The Voice

Around the corner from an abandoned crack house
Folks gathered together in grief

Tears leaned on every available face
Of every different race
Dripping faintly on to the rainy concrete

"Are you fucking kidding me?!," and "Swear to God!"
Twisted off everyone's lips holding no questions or prayers
But rather fears and truths of what we all hoped would never be.

A bitter old black woman who frequents the abandoned crack house walked round wiping tears off strangers'
faces with her bare hands and whispered, "What y'all crying for? We lost her years ago."

Passing vehicles had her voice on repeat like a lonely lover on Valentine's Day

Old gay men described her as
The voice that cradled Mariah in one arm
While catching the door once held open by Aretha with the other.

The bright sun,
The tallest mountain in the valley
The bird caged by the demons of substance abuse

Was humbly gone.

Our sister, our aunt, our cousin, our mother, our beloved had been taken from us
And we no longer had any one to always love us.

I HOPE NOBODY AIN'T ROB ME!

Ima little pissed that I keep losing shit
I lost my headphones twice
I never know where I placed my keys
I be like

"I know I put them in my goddamn bag,
I hope nobody ain't rob me!"

But, I'm always losing shit!
I'm good with holding other people shit but when it comes to me...
I gotta be extra careful
Because I lose things like childhood
Like childhood, I hope nobody ain't rob me.

In and Out

I've been in and out of loving me.

You know
If I had the recipe for it I would follow it.
I would bottle it.
Spill a little in my tea in the morning
Spread a little on my sandwich at lunch
And for dinner, I would prop it up on a pillow and drink myself to death.

I've been in and out of loving me

Imagine

Imagine
Having to give yourself a daily dose of
"It's not you it's them"
Just to keep from mentally beating yourself up when
You know deep down inside you are not to blame

But unfortunately,
A loved one just won't get yo' pain

Fagg*t

Man..I'll tell you.

Gay people get called:
"Faggot"
"Battymon"
"Fish "
"Blade"
"Bulldozer" and "Dike"
Every-fucking-day.

They say:
"Walk like a man"
"Talk like a man"
"Act like a man"
"Put some base in yo' voice!"

Well DAMN!
I gotta do all that?
So you motherfuckers can walk around feeling like you all-at?
Y'all shame us for walking in our truth
And what do we get?
Swagger-jackd by str8 boys wearing skinny jeans and rompers—
NOW-AINT-THAT-A-BITCH?!

You see we "fags"
That is until yo' ass needs the updated fads
And that's when respect seems to become relevant
But the fact that y'all some ignorant motherfuckers is irrelevant—
It's clear that yo' str8 ass don't even know
That gays are the CEOs
To the companies of the latest trends y'all following.

But
Why is it that "gays" are the ones crazy or confused?
When it ain't us with the homophobic issues?

Bit*h

She's angry
She's mad
She's a "black bitch"
All of that because she won't submit?

To the nonsense you list
As she switches her hips
Complimenting her lips,
As you grab on yo' dick
Screaming "fuck you hoe!"
When she does not slow down
To stop
And respond to the bull shit that you bark.

So, the question becomes
"Who *you* callin' a bitch?" (U.N.I.T.Y.)
Her description is too magical to fit your tongue or lips!

So you howl slick shit as she walks on by
Holding her head high
Trying not to cry from all the battles she's fighting on the inside…
She needed that "Hello, good morning my queen,"
But you took the opposite road and cursed at her in screams!

I am the kind

I am the kind who wears a dress,
Next day a suit and heels
No shirt, no shave, bare chest.
I am the kind who minds what's mine
And what's mine is in my mind.
I am the kind that has no limits
While pretending to have boundaries-endless.
I am the kind to slow a room
Entering in a fast-walk, slow-talk, and shining-dark hue.
I am the kind that will call you on yo' shit
Then hand you a scooper and plastic bag so you can trash it.
I am the kind to forgive
And bring that shit up again until you know how it feels.
I am the kind to remind the blind that eye sight
Is just what it is—"sight"
Doesn't mean you can't smell the bullshit.
I am the kind that protects the children,
Educate the ignorant while loving the children.
I am not an apology.
I am not happy.
I am not a fast scream.
I am not a slow cry.
I am not healing.
I am poetry.
I am poetry.
I am poetry.
I am poetry.
I am poetry.
I am poetry.
I am poetry.
I am poetry.
I am poetry.
I. Am. Poetry.

Be Proud of Be Persecuted

When I walk into a room, quietly, listening, for a loving greet
But am welcomed by stares as homophobic pejoratives slip between teeth,
Don't feel sorry for me!
 I'm switching to my own beat.

When I walk into a restroom and they run out,
Making faces
Sneering their noses and twisting their mouths
Scared of how I dress, show up, and be,
Don't feel pity for me!
I like privacy!

When they deny their humanity with me publicly
Simply due to the "codes in the streets,"
Stop! Keep your sympathy!
Don't hurt for me!
I am my own best company.

When I say,
 "Hello, good morning,"
And they twitch their mouths to not respond back
And widen their eyes, disapproving of a man in a dress,
 I just have one request—
 Please don't feel the need to keep me abreast
Of the things they say behind my back once I've left!

When in a room full of people and I'm luxuriating by myself,
Allow me to sit alone—
I don't need your chattering help.
I'm listening to my own self.

They may say, "You do too much!"
They may say, "You act funny!"
They may say, "You talk funny."
They may say, "You walk funny."
They may say, "You need to tone it down; it's not safe to be acting like that 'round here."
And before you know it
"'Round here"
Turns into "everywhere."
So my advice to you:
Just keep on living and doing what you do
Because despite someone else's bullshit, the choice is up to you—

It's either you be proud or be persecuted.

Top of yo' list

Hey,
It's me... Do you not remember?
That day it rained and you offered me your umbrella?
I had on dark green rain boots
And you was lookin' fly as fuck
In ya chucks
Matchin' ya blue suit.
"Shoot!"
You screamed when I said my name was "Lester,"
And you responded, "Nice to meet you, Chester."
You caught a cab, forgetting your umbrella I had and
Sad, I was...
You was gone
And the thought of love was out of fucks to give, but remember this:
When we bumped into each other while waiting for the train on 14th street, we spoke the whole ride,
Sighed about rap not sounding the same
Joyed on Mary J. Blige creating the bible for internal pain...
Until your stop came.
You folded your newspaper and tucked it under your arm
And swung your messenger bag on your back,
And just like that—
The feeling of hopelessness was back!
Until I saw you again, holding her hand, and you smiled at me.
"Oh damn," I whispered.
How could I have mistaken this married straight man for a possible lover?
Something *more* than a passing friend?
And then I responded,
"Hey friend."
And in that moment, just then,
I realized this:
Maybe, possibly, if I were a woman...
I'd be at the top of yo' list.

I love you, anyways

I know you've been taught that big and black is scary, that being gay is a sin, and if I don't repent before the clock strikes life, I'll reside in the pits of Hell. I know you've been taught that going against the odds of fashion means that I'm a bastard, and my father must be to blame. I know you've been taught to believe that if I lose too much weight I must have AIDS, yet with all of this hateful "knowledge"…

I must relay this:

"I love you, anyways ♥"

Till tomorrow,
When we are reminded of the worlds sorrow.

PS: When you wake up in the morning, make sure you say "hello,"
And be thankful to have laid sin free, propped on a sacred pillow.

Stomach

Stomach big
Heavy
Stomach aches
From eating too much but
Stomach can't stop filling itself
Stomach stops me from feeling beautiful
Stomach decides if he could stomach me
To fuck me
Stomach filled with stretch marks and no children insight or children grown now
Stomach sits in lap while driving making the wheel hard to reach
Stomach isn't considered to be related to the mental but is a million-dollar industry
Stomach is always my daily revolution but
Stomach gives me that good stuff, good pain feeling to keep a bitch up off of me
Stomach hides behind plastic wrap, belts, stretch fabric
Stomach ain't appropriate to wear out in public so I hide stomach like a midnight snack
Stomach is mine, I ain't ever proud
I wish
I could douse my stomach in gasoline and watch it burn off me
I wish I could throw my whole body away
I wish my fingernails grew switch blades and would slice my stomach open
I wish my nails could peel back my skin and grind my flesh into chop meat
I wish my stomach had a neck so I could tie a rope around it and choke that shit to death
Every time I think I am something beautiful to lust at I look down at my stomach
Any time I have to remove my shirt in public I damn near throw up at the sight of someone sighting my stomach
Any time I go to a pool and they blow that whistle for me to remove my shirt with all those eyes looking at me
I get pissed the fuck off cause my
Stomach big
Heavy
Stomach aches,
Aches,
Aches,
Breaks,
Like Hearts,
Stomach?

Untitled

I feel: violated, embarrassed
Trapped and boxed in
Like the white casket they buried my mother in
Like that white woman who told me I had charcoal for skin
Like the rapist whom I cherished as a friend
Like the streets and shelters I slept in
Like my father who promised me I'd never see him again.
I feel vulnerable to danger every time I sit and think about myself

Thinking of You

You will miss me most
When I only exist inside your heart
You will call me most
When you say a prayer
You will love me most
When you look at our pictures
And weep.

Winter

The snow has fell
The leaves are gone
Children
Still out to play
But not for long

The season has come
Where we are more alone
Then we are loved.

Where everyone
We have lost
Leaves again

Where trying might end
With life ending
The season has come.

When the leaves might grow
To only fall dead on muddy pillows
And blackbirds will fly to a place
Where only white doves will find grace
The moment is here

Still hoping to be traced
And caught on the journey to happiness and love
The season has come

Where we are more alone
Then we are loved.

Runith Ova'

Who is Michelle Obama before marriage?
Who is Oprah without a dime?
Who was Aretha with no voice?
What is a Christian with no religion?
What is Buddhism without a mantra?
What is America without clean water?
Have you ever wondered?

This poem is for Flint.

The future is dying. Being poisoned.

What's happening?

For Gia, Ifeoma, Nikki G and women everywhere

Sleeping, Dreaming
Mid-afternoon
Exhausted from working
I looked on Facebook
And wrote this moment for you

Daughter what I know is
When the wind blows
And the trees lean
Men reach through and take things:
They take things as a joke
They take things whole
And bring em back broke

And broken

They take things to stray places
And leave em in hope
She'll wind up in a place to be
Absolutely Nobody

But you give, sister,
And it's nothing wrong with givin'
For,
It is not the child who must watch out for the buses
But the buses who must watch out for the child.

All while, warning street signs are necessary.

Mommy's Baby <3

Her mother's insults funded her depression
Till it became so rich that any hope for
Her self-esteem had been bankrupt.

Our love was a joke that went too far:

A quick flight of flirtation that landed in sex.
Our love wasn't broke—
It had way more than enough money
But it could not buy enough tissue to wipe up these hurricane tears
Our hearts shared the same vehicle, but it could not hold an ounce of gasoline
Our trust had a leak
And was running on empty

When I was starving for love

Because you grabbed
My leg
While driving

Because you ritually
Waked me with prayer
Of "good morning babe"

Because you kissed me
Proudly
For all to adore

A poem exhaled
Down my heart
Flow out my nervous system
And landed in
My pen just
For you.

TheLoverPurple

Celie
Was right to LOVE Shug and

Shug
Was right to be SCARED of

LOVING her back

These Days

These days I am somewhere new within myself.
I can't explain
I don't have the vocabulary.
It's a smoother language.
It slides out one's throat, splashes in midair, and is cushioned with a smile.

These days I am doubting less.
Crying more.
Smiling quicker.
Frowning slower.

These days I am running into men that don't understand or want to comprehend that I am human. That I have
feelings and need healing
Too.
I want some-*thingz*, but these days I don't need much.

These days
I'm appreciating my gut
Bouncing my butt
Oiling my skin
Standing in the sun longer
And wearing clothes that fit me (with a little extra room).

I can eat and let my belly hang
I can cough and let my back expand
Wear shoes that I can:
Run in
March in
Stand in
Sit in
At any given moment

This poem will and can go on
but bottom line: for me
In this moment,
On this day,
In this floral sour hour
I'm here.
I'm human.
I'm living
Like a mind wrapped up in dreadlocks ready to blow locks

I'm here.

But We Can Be Friends

I'm sorry for lying to you.

It's not that I had to work
I wasn't sick last Friday
My cousin never had an emergency
My car never stopped working
My phone didn't die
I had great service
I been saw your text
And unfortunately,
What's true of all the lies I told you is:
"I really don't have another boo"

"I thought I was dropping clues'
"I didn't mean to confuse you"

It's just, I'm not that in to you.

Old Folks,

They were here first
They dreamt first
They failed first
They loved first
They hurt first
They succeeded first
They fucked up first
They got it wrong first
They got it right first
They marched first
They drowned first
They were ignorant first
They know a lot first and sometimes
They don't know shit at all.
Old folks are human and you'll be an old folk soon and an old folk will be you.

Everything Ain't Just Black and White

I know,
That her booty defines her beauty
That if given the opportunity
She would claim to the highest pain of slave names

She wishes history (without its truthful pain) would offer over its effortless beauty

She wishes:
To be darker
But not too dark
With thicker flesh
But with no lashes
Lips thicker
But not painted like bamboos
In the New York Times cartoons
She wants to be black

 But not the color purple Black
Not Black, Black
Nah, she wants to be black
Like White-black

Definition:
adjective
    1. 1.
People of the African diaspora features are only deemed beautiful by the privileged race, when most opportune to them.
verb
    1. 1.
 Black beauty compartmentalized.

Listen,

Do not be chained to the idea that parents are the sole definition of your existence
Do not be wedded to the rubric of religion, guiding the way and how you love
Do not find yourself marrying into convince or having sex out of vengefulness

Come out from behind that pulpit
Rise up out of that Temple
Teachers,
Leave the chalk at the chalkboard, sit down
And allow the children to teach about being free.

We don't know everything.

I call upon every child and everybody with a child spirit, to come forth, and lead us, to freedom.
I call upon every child and everybody with a child spirit, to come forth, and lead us, to freedom.
I call upon every child and everybody with a child spirit, to come forth, and lead us, to freedom.
I call upon every child and everybody with a child spirit, to come forth, and lead us, to freedom.
I call upon every child and everybody with a child spirit, to come forth, and lead us, to freedom.
I call upon every child and everybody with a child spirit, to come forth, and lead us, to freedom.
I call upon every child and everybody with a child spirit, to come forth, and lead us, to freedom.
I call upon every child and everybody with a child spirit, to come forth, and lead us, to freedom.
I call upon every child and everybody with a child spirit, to come forth, and lead us, to freedom.
I call upon every child and everybody with a child spirit, to come forth, and lead us, to freedom.
I call upon every child and everybody with a child spirit, to come forth, and lead us, to freedom. .

11/29/1994

I was born on the day my father died.
That is, he went to the store for milk
Hours before my mother went into labor,
And never came back again.

?

When I think of myself and all the people I help,
I always think about who will help me?

Better yet,
Who will love me?

And for how long?

Untiled 2

He walked in with pride, but it was obvious he was a troubled man: sorry clouded his pupils and the trapped heavy tear drops **contributed** to his inability **to** make direct eye contact.

Although we sat directly across from each other, **his** toes seemed to be purposely positioned away from my direction as if he was ready to run away or had been running from something.

Something that is his **own**
But it never used to belong to him.

Something that leaves hickeys like an ex-lover
Something that is only exposed under covers

Nothing to gain
But **pain.**

As long as nobody finds out.

That his lover shares a physical commonality.

By living in other people's opinions. He contributed to his own pain.

9pm

Depression was sweet enough to only visit her at night,
When she would fall asleep: it was her melatonin, Benadryl and bedtime tea.

Most nights, *depression* would violate her state of fullness after eating dinner
And rape her hungry.

She'd lay in bed nibbling her feelings away,
Until the mattress began to blend in with the shape of her body.
She laid there, dreading the day.

She wanted so badly to be released from the fear:
That there is no human being healed enough to value the truth of her,
That she deserves to be loved without envy.
She wants to be desired and to be explored in random dreams
And researched in philosophical poetry.

You Know Who You Are

You have to live with what you did to me
But hopefully
You'll never have to live what you did to me.

I forgive you.

Untiled 3

"A rapist doesn't have to be a stranger to be considered legitimate."- Ntozake Shange

It is always disappointing when we find out that our father's, brothers, uncles, husbands and cousins
Whom of which we have cherished like a sunflower or a white rose from birth
Turns out to be a dead cactus
Sticking their limped spikes in places they don't belong
In random places with no permission.

Not strangers
But our very own flesh and blood
They too are capable of violating the innocent.

The only way to be deceived, is to trust.

K

I hope that number one:
Love is meant for me
I hope that number two:
Whoever that love might be
Is as good, sweet and good looking as you.

Brother

I cannot describe how hurt I was when you wished me to hell
After you claimed my safety in your hands like God on a Sunday.

I believed that you are destined for more than you allow yourself to believe
Than demons of substance abuse will allow you to achieve.

Brother, I do not know why I am writing this poem
Or why this poem is writing 'WE'.

I do not think I can verbally say this
So instead I write to you:

That I love you brother, forever, even with all that we've gone through.

Purse

She walks with her purse tucked under her arm in case a mother fucker tries to snatch it.
In case she has to check them bastards for disrespecting her.
In case she has to feed any child, she sees during day and night.
In case she has to choke one up to do right.
She's never done!

She's the mother fucking QUEEN, Elizabeth ain't got shit on her!
She walks with her purse tucked under her arm
In case she has to pull out those lyrics to a funeral song
In case a trusted friend tries to slide up her thighs when nighttime rise
In case she has to send a visitor home with three shoes on from kicking up in his ass
In case this WORLD needs reminding of her existence…

You see,
She walks with her purse tucked under her arm in case a mother fucker tries to snatch her…

Smokin No Mo

Man I wish my brother wasn't smokin no more.
Because if he wasn't smokin no mo!
Yo, don't you know that he would probably be one of the greatest reporters you'll see on TV!
He'd be on ABC, NBC oh yes! even MTV.
He would definitely be the epitome of what a great journalist is supposed to be, if he wasn't smokin No mo!

Always two steps ahead of the rest
He would be totally dedicated to keeping us abreast of Current events, honorable mention, speaking at conventions and generating attention, able to face the toughest crowds without flinchin carefully choosing words, beautifully spoken if he wasn't smokin!

Man, I wish my sister wasn't smokin no more!
Because she looks so much different than she did befo!
Her skin used to have such a beautiful glow she don't even comb her hair no mo!
She just stays up just geekin for weeks in a row and you know her opinion of herself is low
Because she doing all kinds of shit she never did befo!
And doing all these things ain't gonna do nothing but bring her self-esteem way way way down low! Till she'll have to look up just see the floor!

And the shit won't stop there you know because once it gets started it just likes to go and before long it really starts to show how you losing your power and your spirit is broken! Oh lord have mercy I, I wish she wasn't smokin no mo.

Man I wish my mamma wasn't smokin no mo.
Cause I get tired of crying for her when she gets tired of trying for her, her spirit slowly dying and her attitude defiantly lacking gratitude. Sometimes becoming down right rude the shit just takes her through so many moods, she's hardly eating any food.
Fuck nutrition! Because every day and every night she's on a whole other mission and once again I'm right back to wishing Damn!
I wish she only listened.

Can't she see how much I'm missing...spending time with her kickin it the bow bow.
She used to like K-C!
I used to like Jojo!
Together we was hoping they would never go solo be like Al Green and stay together
Aot like Puffy and JLo.
But that was our dreams way back in the day tho befo you know?

All I can do is keep praying and coping.
Giving you love and support and keep hoping you keep your mind open to what you can do
And take back your power when you're ready to!
And when that does happened you'll feel what I'm saying,

You'll take me more seriously and "no" I ain't playing!
You need to keep praying and staying in touch
I'm always gonna be here and I love you that much!

But lookin at your life it fills me with a hard to shake feeling...I...I...I I'm filled with emotion Sometimes I can't talk cause my tears got me chokin!
I can't do my job I'm supposed to be jokin!

But god
It's so hard
When you love somebody
Somebody whose smokin.

WHAT IS POETRY?

Poetry, will not let me sleep
It won't let me think
About anything
Not even about me
It demands just as much truth as a new born demands from their parents
And rightfully so.
Poetry is not written on demand
It is created out of grave plots and birth out of hearts living in tyranny and truth.
Poetry is not manufactured it's:
Fat
Ugly
Skinny
Pretty
Poor
Rich
Plain
Fly
Gay
Bi
Man
Woman
Non-binary
Gender fluid
Trans
And things we have yet to identify with.
Poetry is worth life and so are you.

YOU ARE POETRY.

This How I Talk

"This how I talk."
Even though I know it's not grammatically correct
That don't make me no difference; I just need you to respect
The way I say what I say when I talk every day.
Even though I may not speak for effect,
This how I talk...

We live in a country that's so full of shit,
So don't criticize me 'cause I can't get with:
Yo' grammer, yo' lingo, yo' doing yo' thang, oh
I'm wrong 'cause I like *Empire* and yo' ass like the *GoldBergs*—oh no I don't think so.
This how I talk...

You think I'm gon listen to people like you
When I see, hear, and read all the shit that you do:
The same country that exploits us and uses our skills for profit and gain
But our brothers they kill
And my naïve sisters you manipulate so well
Need to just wear a sign saying "sex for sale,"
But only corporate pimps will make an attempt to market their product, and they do it well,
'Cause if you sell yo' own body, yo' ass gon to jail.
This how I talk...

Just 'cause I don't say it how you tell me I *should*
That don't make what I'm saying misunderstood.
I talk like I wanna—I'm just being me—I feel justified and I just feel so free
'Cause I've experienced up close your hypocrisy when you stole away my identity
Then told me that I'm supposed to be me
Then tried to trick a bitch by telling me I'm free.
This how I talk.

And this how it's gonna be. Until you can explain to me some foul shit about you,
I'ma talk just the way that I choose to...

You see, I really don't think you've got my best interest at heart, and
I'm not being rebellious—I'm just being smart
'Cause its really not easy to live in a nation that's okay with welfare and not reparation
Trapping you in a system and calling it help. Shit, just open up the door and I'll get it myself.

This how I talk, and this all I got left: to say what I wanna and in my own way,
And I'ma utilize this right while I got it today
'Cause if the right people get pissed, they gon take that away:

Don't forget that in schools it's illegal to pray.

Don't hate on me 'cause I call what I see.
Just don't fear the truth, 'cause it will set you free
But that freedom we speak of, it comes with a price.
Don't lose your strength 'cause you tryna be nice; go ahead and piss somebody off
Once or twice—
I guarantee you it'll be worth the sacrifice.
This how I talk...

The junkies, the dealers in my neighborhood
Y'all stressin' in the news that they ain't no good,
but what I never hear about is how they could
have access to millions in trafficking goods
when most of these people never leave the neighborhood.

But as soon as little rich suburbanites mimic,
You're screaming on the TV, "The shit's epedimic."
It wasn't a problem as long as it stayed in the streets and the parks where the dark
Children played.

This how I talk, and I wont shut up until those
In power realize we've had enough—
I'm tired.

Tired of seeing the same shit on the news everyday;
I'm tired of hearing the perpetrator got suspended with pay—
That's a fucking vacation (if we gon keep this real)—
Tired of knowing they don't give a damn how we feel.

This how I talk. You better learn to respect that
It ain't about ignorance
It's about dialect.
To me it's called flava, now
Where your flava at?
I talk like I wanna. I don't need yo' permission. Don't be trippin'
'Cause I end a sentence with a preposition.

This how I talk, and
"No I'm not high." This how I talk.
Fuck it, this just how I cry!!!!!!!!

Lester Mayers is a Brooklyn native who is currently completing his undergraduate degree in Theatre Performance at SUNY New Paltz School of Fine and Performing Arts. Lester is a published writer, poet and actor. In 2017 Lester won the SUNY Chancellors awards for artistic excellence. His work can be found in the Sojourner Truth Library, I am from Driftwood LGBTQ archive, and the Huffington Post. Lester's performance credits includes: SUNY Oswego, SUNY FLCC, Pace University, SUNY UB, and countless others. Gay, black, feminine, and a feminist, Lester tackles issues that have historically been ignored by the public.

Lester's unique, truthful artistry expands beyond poetry and writing. He starred in SUNY New Paltz's sold out 2017 production of "To Kill A Mockingbird" and the 2012 Pulitzer winning play 'Water by the Spoonful' in 2018. He also narrated the 2016 Finger Lakes Community College children theater tour production of "Miss Electricity." He is a street trained hip-hop dancer/choreographer and work has been featured in the Nike Step it Up Dance Competition, Dr Oz South Street Seaport Dance Competition, and his choreography has ranked number one multiples times in the New York Division of All Stars Dance Competition. Lester believes in no boxes, no artistic labels and giving his all every step of the way.

Made in the USA
Middletown, DE
06 March 2019